The House on Jacob Street

Written by Barbara Moore

Illustrated by Chantal Stewart

sundance

a black dog book

Published by
Sundance Publishing
P.O. Box 1326
234 Taylor Street
Littleton, MA 01460

Copyright © text Barbara Moore
Copyright © illustrations Chantal Stewart

First published 2001 by
Pearson Education Australia Pty. Limited
95 Coventry Street
South Melbourne 3205 Australia
Exclusive United States Distribution: Sundance Publishing

ISBN 0-7608-4976-5

Printed in China

Contents

Characters

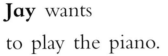

Jay wants
to play the piano.

Clara loves
beautiful music and
beautiful flowers.

Chapter One

Jay's Secret

Jay had a secret. Each night he wished for a piano. He lay awake and looked at the stars. He imagined himself playing the piano. He would sit on a velvet bench and study the music. Then he would sit up straight and begin to play.

He imagined touching the smooth black and white keys. He could almost hear the crisp sound of the notes he would play. He imagined being a famous piano player.

He often asked his mom and dad if they could buy a piano. But the answer was always the same.

"We can't afford a piano, Jay," said his mom.

"Please," Jay pleaded. "What about a little one?"

"Maybe next year, Jay," said his dad. "Then you can even have lessons."

Chapter Two
Jacob Street

Every day, Jay walked home from school, sometimes with friends, sometimes alone. Every day, he walked along Main Street, past the stores, past the bakery, past the library, and past the florist, until he got to Jacob Street.

But Jay didn't notice much while he walked and whistled. He was always daydreaming about making beautiful music on his imaginary piano.

Every day, before Jay reached a certain house, he crossed the road. He didn't like going by the scary house on Jacob Street. It was old and dark and creepy.

Even the yard of the scary house was creepy. Weeds gripped the sidewalk. Vines strangled the fence. And the ivy tangled around the gate in a very spooky way.

Each time Jay passed the scary house, he trembled with fear. Who would live in a house like that?

Chapter Three
The Open Window

One day, Jay wandered home from school. He was lost in his favorite daydream. It was the one where he comes home to find a glossy, black piano delivered to his door. Down the street he wandered, dreaming of the music he would play, and the melodies he would compose on his piano.

Jay was so busy daydreaming that he forgot to cross the street. Before he knew it, he was right outside the scary house on Jacob Street—alone!

For a moment, he froze. He could see
the strangling vines, the tangled ivy, and
the weeds gripping the sidewalk.

Jay was terrified.

Then he heard a sound. A beautiful sound. A musical sound.

He stood and listened. The sound filled the air all around him. Then silence. Jay lifted his head and heard it again.

The beautiful sound came from the house on Jacob Street—the scary house on Jacob Street.

The music was like a magnet drawing him in. It pulled him toward the old fence, the old gate, and the sidewalk covered with vines and weeds.

Jay opened the gate. He certainly was
scared, but the sound drew him closer and
closer. He trudged through the tangled
vines and trees to an open window.

Chapter Four
The Piano

Jay peeked in the window. He could see
a magnificent room. The walls were
covered in paintings. A crystal chandelier
hung from the ceiling. Hundreds of tiny
lights twinkled down. The room wasn't
scary. Not one little bit.

A piano stood in the corner. It was the most beautiful piano Jay had ever seen.

16

A woman was playing the piano. She was looking out the open window, right at Jay.

Jay froze again. This time, he was too scared to move.

Slowly, the woman got up from the bench and came to the window. Jay wanted to run away. But he was still too scared to move.

"Hello," said the woman. "Who are you? And what are you doing outside my window?" She didn't sound angry. And she didn't look mean. She looked...nice.

"It was the music," whispered Jay. His voice was so soft. It could hardly be heard.

The woman stared at Jay for a minute, then her face crinkled up in a smile. "Do you like music?" she asked.

Jay came closer. He tried to speak. "If I had a piano like yours..." he whispered. But he couldn't finish the sentence. How could he tell this woman that her piano was just like the one in his dream?

"Do you have a piano?" she asked.

"I've given up asking for one," said Jay.

"Would you like to play my piano?"
said the woman.

Jay couldn't believe it.

Then Jay's heart sank. "I don't know how to play the piano," he said. "I only dream about playing."

"Oh well," said the woman. "Maybe one day. I'm Clara. What's your name?"

"Jay," he answered.

Chapter Five
The Deal

Jay ran home as fast as he could. He couldn't wait to tell his parents what had happened at the scary house.

"Her name is Clara," Jay blurted out as soon as he rushed in the door. "And she lives in the scary house on Jacob Street. She plays the most beautiful piano."

But Jay's parents didn't seem surprised at all. "Oh, Clara's back, is she? We should visit her. You know, Jay, Clara is a very famous pianist."

Jay couldn't believe his luck. His parents knew Clara!

"Clara has always lived in that old house," said Jay's dad.

"Maybe she knows someone who teaches piano," said his mom.

"Could I go back to see her in the morning?" said Jay. "I'd like to ask Clara to teach me."

And that's just what Jay did.

The next morning, he went straight back to the scary house on Jacob Street. He walked right up the sidewalk and knocked at the door.

When Clara came to the door, she was
still in her robe.

Jay got straight to the point. "Good
morning, Clara," he said. "I can do yard
work. I can weed and dig and trim. Would
you please teach me to play the piano?"

Clara thought for a moment. She looked carefully at Jay.

After what seemed like a long time, she smiled. "It would be my pleasure to teach you, Jay," she said. "You have a deal."

Jay blinked hard. Maybe this was another daydream. It was like the daydream where a piano is delivered. Only this dream was even better. And it really was happening.

Chapter Six

Beautiful Music

Now, every day, Jay walks home from school, sometimes with friends and sometimes alone. But now, every day, Jay doesn't cross the road. He goes straight to the scary house. He walks right through the gate and straight to the door. He carries his music under his arm. And Clara is always there to greet him.

Jay and Clara sit together on the velvet piano bench. They study the music. Then Jay sits up straight and begins to play.

He touches the smooth black and white keys. He hears the crisp sound of the notes. He imagines being a famous piano player.

Every weekend, Jay and Clara pull out weeds. Or they trim the vines or cut back the ivy, to keep a clear path to the door. One special weekend, they planted tiny lavender bushes.

Now those plants have grown. A line of
beautiful, blue bushes leads the way to the
front door of the house on Jacob Street.

All around the house on Jacob Street, you can hear the sound of Jay and Clara playing piano together. And all around the neighborhood, people call it the beautiful house on Jacob Street.